Hush, Little Trucker

words by Kim Norman

pictures by Toshiki Nakamura

ABRAMS APPLESEED
NEW YORK

For Paisley, Kristi, and Tanya, because girls love trucks, too!
—K.N.

For Mom and Dad
—T.N.

The illustrations in this book were created digitally.

Cataloging-in-Publication Data has been applied for and may be obtained from the Library of Congress.

ISBN 978-1-4197-4644-4

Text © 2021 Kim Norman
Illustrations © 2021 Toshiki Nakamura
Book design by Hana Anouk Nakamura

Printed and bound in China
10 9 8 7 6 5 4 3 2

For bulk discount inquiries, contact specialsales@abramsbooks.com.

ABRAMS The Art of Books
195 Broadway, New York, NY 10007
abramsbooks.com

Hush, little trucker, you're in luck.

Mama's gonna find your lost toy truck.

But if that toy truck's sunk too deep . . .

we'll close our eyes and shout "beep, beep!"

And when we open up our eyes . . .

POOF! There's a jeep that's just our size!

And if that jeep gets stranded in a drift,

we're gonna climb on a tall forklift.

And if that lift's two forks get stuck,

let's take a ride on a wide dump truck.

And if that dump truck just won't go,
we'll root around with a strong backhoe.

And if that backhoe still won't fix 'er,

let's fire up a concrete mixer.

And if that mixer won't roll around,

we're gonna bulldoze a mighty mound.

And if that dozer digs up muck,

we'll haul it off with a flatbed truck.

And if that truck's got a broken motor,

let's blaze a trail with a front-end loader.

**And if that loader heaves and strains,
you'll take command of a giant crane.**

And if that crane is much too big,

we'll turn it off and start to dig.

And when, through the snow, comes a flash of blue,
you'll shout "Hooray!" and . . .

"I love you!"